Beware of the Blabbermouth!

Find out more spooky secrets about

Ghostville Elementary®

...tville Elementary®

Beware of the Blabbermouth!

by **Marcia Thornton Jones**
and
Debbie Dadey

illustrated by **Guy Francis**

———

A
LITTLE APPLE
PAPERBACK

New York   Sydney
Mexico City   New Delhi   Hong Kong   Buenos Aires

To, of course, "Lewonnie" (otherwise known as Lewanna Sexton and Bonnie Hall) — who can blab all they want to! Thanks for the laughter!

— MTJ

To the Arsenal Blue Team of Becky Dadey, Annie Baker, Paige Denke, Karsynn Miller, Lindsay Pfankuch, Elke Zeuner, Aubrey Eder, Gabby Laureles, Amber Scheaffer, Ashley Chavez, Peyton Stouffer, Taylor Mares, Catie Fossy, Danyelle Minchow, and Leah Clark.

— DD

ISBN 0-439-68120-0

Text copyright © 2004 by Marcia Thornton Jones and Debra S. Dadey. Illustrations copyright © 2004 by Scholastic Inc. SCHOLASTIC, LITTLE APPLE, GHOSTVILLE ELEMENTARY, and associated logos are trademarks and/or registered trademarks of Scholastic Inc.

12 11 10 9 8 7 6 5 4 3 2 1   4 5 6 7 8 9/0

Printed in the U.S.A.   40
First printing, November 2004

Contents

THE LEGEND

Sleepy Hollow Elementary School's
Online Newspaper

This Just In: The third graders in the basement may never have recess again!

Breaking News: Someone has been writing awful stuff about the whole third grade. I don't know why. I don't know how. But if the dirty, rotten tattletale isn't caught soon, the third graders may never see the light of day again. Hey, maybe that's how the basement got haunted in the first place! So long, third graders. Hello, ghosts!

Stay tuned for more breaking news.

Your friendly fifth-grade reporter,
Justin Thyme

1
Ghost Boogers

NINA PICKS HER NOSE

The words were written in orange chalk under the old map that hung on the chalkboard. Everyone saw them as soon as Darla raised the map.

Carla tugged on Mr. Morton's necktie. "Somebody . . ."

". . . wrote on the board," her twin sister finished. Carla and Darla made a habit of keeping Mr. Morton informed.

"Nina picks her slimy boogers," Andrew said with a laugh.

"It's not true!" Nina mumbled. She felt her face turning red, so she hid it behind her long black hair. Nina hated being the shortest one in the class, but just then she wanted to be so short she could

1

shrink into her desk. The whole class smiled as Mr. Morton hurried to erase the big letters on the board.

Carla grabbed the eraser first. "Let us . . ."

". . . take care of it," Darla said. She picked up another eraser and turned the words into a gigantic orange smear.

"Thanks," Mr. Morton said with a smile. "You girls are lifesavers." Then he handed them each a gold star. Carla and

Darla hurried to stick the stars on the covers of their journals. Their notebooks sparkled with all the stickers they had collected from Mr. Morton.

Cassidy reached across the aisle and patted Nina on the arm. "It's okay," Cassidy whispered.

"Nobody cares," Jeff added. Jeff, Cassidy, and Nina were good friends. They always stuck up for one another. No matter what.

Nina had only picked her nose once at school and that's when she'd been the last one in the classroom. Nobody had seen. At least she didn't think they had.

Carla and Darla snickered and looked at Nina. In fact, everyone in the class laughed except for Nina's two good friends. Well, that wasn't exactly true. Several blobs of green haze took shape at the back of the room near Nina's desk. The green blobs didn't laugh, either.

They had mischief on their minds. Ghost mischief.

Sleepy Hollow Elementary was nick-named Ghostville Elementary for a very good reason. When their school became so crowded that the third-grade class-room was forced to move into the base-ment, Jeff, Cassidy, and Nina had found out the horrible truth. The rumors about ghosts were true. Even worse, the ghosts only appeared to the three of them. Nina was sure the rest of the class would have screamed if they'd seen the ghosts ap-pearing out of the swirling haze.

Nate, a quiet ghost, floated through the air until he was so close to Nina she had to turn her head to keep him from peer-ing up her nose.

Ozzy was not the nicest ghost in the world. He stood at the front of the room and pretended to pick his own nose while his sister, Becky, watched. Of course, he grew his nose to be as big as a watermelon. Nina's stomach tumbled at the thought of ghost boogers stuck in there.

Sadie was the only ghost who didn't seem to find boogers the least bit funny. Sadie was never very happy, but now she was downright upset. She pulled at her long stringy hair and pointed at Nina's nose. "Nooooooo," she moaned. Nina was thankful that the rest of the classroom ghosts hadn't shown up to tease her.

The ghosts in the classroom didn't giggle or snicker or chuckle. They howled with laughter. Their voices blended until it sounded like a truck bearing down on the classroom. Of course, only Nina, Cassidy, and Jeff heard the noise since ghosts didn't let just anybody hear them.

It was bad enough that the entire classroom was making fun of her. Nina didn't need the ghosts howling at her, too. She pressed her hands to her ears and blinked back tears.

Their teacher, Mr. Morton, didn't know

anything about the ghosts, but he did know that making fun of somebody was not a good thing. He rubbed chalk dust from his glasses and gave the class his most serious look.

"I don't know who wrote this," he said firmly, "but it better not happen again!"

2
Killer Rabbit

"Did you see that movie last night?" Jeff asked Cassidy and Nina as they came back into their classroom after lunch. "Creatures from the Black Lagoon terrorized a town."

Nina shuddered. "That sounds slimy and icky."

"Sort of like your boogers," Andrew said from behind them. Andrew always seemed to show up at the wrong time. Which was every time, if you asked Nina.

Jeff ignored Andrew. "I wish I knew what movie makeup they use for the special effects. I'd make myself into a creature." Jeff planned on making scary movies when he grew up. He was an expert on the kinds of ghosts, goblins, and monsters that appeared on film.

Jeff didn't notice that the rest of the class was clustered at the front of the room. Cassidy did. She tugged on Jeff's sleeve until he stopped talking. Jeff slowly turned to see a message scratched in blue letters across Mr. Morton's flip chart.

JEFF IS AFRAID OF BUNNIES!

Andrew hopped around Jeff. "Look out!" Andrew said between laughs. "My little bunny whiskers might poke you to death."

Jeff remembered looking up movies on the classroom computer a few days ago when everyone else was finishing their double-digit multiplication problems. A poster for an old movie called *Killer Rabbit* had popped up on the screen so suddenly it had startled him. He might

have jumped a little bit, but nobody had seen him. Nobody.

Mr. Morton clapped his hands until the class stopped laughing. "Some species of rabbits can get rather large," their teacher started to say.

"Like the Easter Bunny!" Andrew blurted out.

The class burst into laughter again. This time, no amount of clapping could make them stop.

Darla rushed to the chart. "Let us . . ."

". . . help," Carla said. Then they both ripped the page from the chart.

Mr. Morton gave the twins his biggest smile. "If everyone could be half as helpful as Carla and Darla, we would never have these problems," he said as he handed each girl a gold star.

Nina noticed the smart ghost named Edgar oozing out of the picture on the wall to follow Carla and Darla. Usually Nina worried that the ghosts would bother the other kids, but for once she

didn't care. She watched Edgar push Nate aside to hover over the two girls as they carefully placed the new stickers on the covers of their journals. Edgar held his own tattered journal to his chest.

The rest of the ghosts couldn't care less about journals. They seemed to think the idea of Jeff being afraid of a bunny was funny. Becky hopped around Jeff's desk. Ozzy leaped through the air with his hair stuck up like rabbit ears. He looked more like a clumsy frog than a cute bunny. Even Sadie bounced around the room. Only Nate floated quietly around the ceiling.

Jeff's face turned from white to pink to red.

"Your red face won't match your pink bunny nose," Andrew teased. "Hey, will you give me extra chocolate eggs for Easter?"

The rest of the class laughed even harder. Mr. Morton, however, was not amused. "If this happens again," he warned, "nobody will get recess. And I mean *no one*!"

That was enough to quiet the class. Everyone except the ghosts. They still hopped around the room. When Ozzy landed on Jeff's desk, he sent the ghost tumbling with a wave of his hand.

"Ignore them," Nina whispered to Jeff.

"Maybe they'll go away," Cassidy added, but she didn't sound very sure.

There was one thing Ozzy did not like. Being ignored.

3
Bunny Boy

"No," Nina gasped under her breath, but it was no use. Ozzy tipped the potted plant off the window ledge. Dirt and leaves splashed across the classroom floor.

"It must have been the wind," Carla said, since no one was near the plant.

"We'll clean it up," Darla said.

While Carla and Darla swept up the mess, Ozzy flew around the room. He zoomed faster and faster until Nina thought she would throw up. She put her head down on her desk and thought, *Who could be writing all these wild things? Why would anyone do something like that?*

Nina raised her head as Mr. Morton

gave the twins more gold stickers. Edgar floated over to watch.

Nina looked around the room trying to figure out who the tattletale could be.

Jeff wondered the same thing as the kids headed over to his house after school. "Someone's been spying on us," Jeff sputtered as they crossed the street to his driveway. He kicked a deflated soccer ball out of the way and jumped over a tricycle parked on the sidewalk.

Cassidy grinned. "Does that mean you really *are* afraid of fluffy little bunnies?" she asked.

Jeff's face turned red again. "That's not true. I just got startled by a picture of one on a Web site once. Anyone would've jumped."

"And I don't pick my nose," Nina added.

"Never?" Cassidy asked. Nina's eyes narrowed, but Cassidy patted Nina on the shoulder before she could get angrier. "Don't worry. By tomorrow no one will remember a thing."

But rumors at Sleepy Hollow Elementary flew faster than a bat through the midnight sky. By the time

Jeff and his friends got inside his house, it was obvious that it was not just the third graders who knew about the mysterious tattletale. His three sisters knew, too.

Jeff's oldest sister looked up over a fashion magazine she was reading. "Hey, Bunny Boy," Marissa teased him. "Should I go hide all the carrots and lettuce?"

Jeff threw his shoe at Marissa, but she wasn't the only one teasing him. His two little sisters pranced down the stairs wearing cotton bunny tails and hopped in a circle around Jeff.

Jeff started to chase after them, but Cassidy grabbed his arm. "Don't worry about it," she said.

"That's easy for you to say," Jeff huffed.

"No one said anything bad about you." Nina poked her finger at Cassidy.

"Yeah," Jeff added, throwing his book bag in the laundry room and glaring at Cassidy.

Cassidy shrugged. "Somebody played a joke on you both. It was rotten, but it's not the end of the world. Try to forget about it."

But the next morning things went from bad to worse.

4
News Flash

Andrew and a small crowd of kids gathered around the computer in the back of the classroom. Barbara, Allison, and Melissa were giggling and a boy named Randy pointed at the screen and laughed out loud. Even Carla and Darla looked like they were hiding smiles behind their hands.

Justin Thyme and his fifth-grade buddies were in charge of writing and producing the online school newspaper. Usually *The Legend* was filled with articles about special projects and celebrations. Sometimes the fifth-grade writers added pictures to go with the stories. But today the fifth graders had outdone themselves. *The Legend* flashed a BOOGERS AND BUNNIES headline.

"Oh, no!" Nina gasped. "The whole school reads that!"

The hot pink letters flashed like a neon sign and a rabbit hopped across the bottom of the slime-green screen.

"Who did that?" Jeff demanded.

"They're going to pay," Nina added.

"What're you going to do?" Andrew asked. "Hop circles around them while bombarding them with boogers?" Andrew laughed so hard he stumbled backward

and fell right through Edgar. Of course, Andrew didn't know he had tumbled through a ghost since Andrew couldn't see Edgar.

Cassidy ignored Edgar as the ghost put himself back together. "The byline says it was written by Justin Thyme," Cassidy said.

"Aren't newspapers supposed to print the facts and nothing but the facts?" Jeff huffed. "Where did he get this stuff?"

Carla started reading the article. "'According to an unidentified source . . .'"

"'. . . there is breaking news from the basement classroom,'" Darla added.

Nina's bottom lip trembled. She let her dark hair fall down in front of her face so nobody could see her blush. "I can't believe Justin wrote an entire article about Jeff and me," she said.

"He didn't," Darla told her.

"There's more," Carla added.

The kids gathered close to the monitor as the twins read out loud. They weren't the only ones reading. Edgar swooped between the girls as they took turns reading.

Darla read loud and clear, as if she were auditioning for a Broadway play. "'Our reporter in the field has the scoop on several third graders.'"

Carla's voice was just as loud and clear as her sister's. "'Recently, Barbara Murphy was seen swiping potato chips from lunchboxes.'"

Everyone turned and faced Barbara. "That was you?" Andrew asked. "You ate my potato chips?"

Barbara wasn't laughing anymore. She looked from face to face as the other kids glared at her. "I was hungry," she said softly.

"'When Allison Fryer broke Mr. Morton's calculator,'" Darla read on, "'she hid it underneath the scrap paper.'"

"'Mr. Morton looked high and low for it, but he never thought to look there.

Allison didn't think to tell him, either,'" Carla finished.

Allison's face turned the color of fruit juice. "I . . . I . . . I . . . didn't mean to break it," she stammered.

"Busted," Andrew roared. "Busted like Humpty Dumpty!" He pointed at Allison and laughed. "Wait until Mr. Morton finds out!"

A few of the kids giggled, but most of them were quiet now, especially the ones

whose secrets had been splashed across the screen. Carla and Darla kept reading. The more they read, the quieter the group became.

" 'Of course, Andrew Potts has been in rare form,' " Carla read as she scrolled down the screen.

Andrew stopped laughing and pushed Carla away from the screen. "Hey! I'm famous! What does it say about me?" he asked. But when he saw the screen, the smile wilted from his face. "No," he whispered. "No. NO!"

5
Blankie

"What does it say?" Jeff asked, shoving Andrew aside.

"It says," Darla told him, "that Andrew sleeps with a blankie!"

Cassidy couldn't help smiling. After all, Andrew was always picking on other kids.

Jeff noticed Cassidy's smile. "I can't believe it," he said. "You're the unidentified source! You're the one telling everyone's secrets."

"I am not!" Cassidy argued.

Nina's eyes got big. "You *are* the computer expert around here," Nina said quietly. "You could've sent Justin all those things."

But then Cassidy saw the last line of *The Legend* article.

My source also says Cassidy Logan
loves Mr. Morton.

Cassidy flashed her eyes at Jeff. "When I told you I liked him, I didn't mean it *that* way!" she shouted. "How could you write that for everybody to see?"

"I didn't do it!" Jeff yelled back.

"It had to be you," Cassidy snapped. "You're the only one I told."

Then everybody started yelling. Andrew shouted at Jeff. Barbara yelled at Melissa. Allison hollered at everyone. In two seconds, every kid took sides except for Nina, Darla, and Carla. Half of the class stood behind Cassidy and half behind Jeff.

Even the ghosts took sides. A musical ghost named Calliope slid out from behind the bookshelves along with Sadie and Becky. Nate and Ozzy zipped over to

Jeff's side. Nina stood in the middle with the ghost dog, Huxley, trembling by her knees and Cocomo the ghost cat sitting on her shoes. Edgar stayed out of the way. He perched on top of his favorite picture frame, his plain brown journal in hand, watching everyone else fight.

"You better . . ." Carla started.

". . . stop fighting," Darla added. "It's against the rules."

"Aw, be quiet," Randy snapped at Carla.

"We've had enough of you two," Andrew shouted.

Mr. Morton rushed into the room at that exact moment looking as if he had just tumbled out of bed. Carla and Darla immediately told him about the online newspaper article.

Mr. Morton clapped for silence, but nobody paid attention. He dug through the bottom drawer of his desk until he found a whistle. Then he blew it long and loud until everyone, even the ghosts, covered their ears.

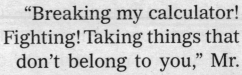

"Breaking my calculator! Fighting! Taking things that don't belong to you," Mr. Morton said. "It seems as if nobody has been following rules except, of course, Carla and Darla!"

Jeff and Cassidy glared at each other.

"Andrew just slept with an itty-bitty baby blankie," Randy said in his most innocent voice. "He didn't break any rules."

Andrew curled his fingers into a fist. "I'll break something. You just wait until recess," he said to Randy.

Mr. Morton put a hand between Andrew and Randy. "If you're waiting for recess, you have a long wait, because *nobody* is going to recess."

Carla batted her eyelashes. "But we didn't . . ."

31

"... do anything wrong," Darla added.

Mr. Morton smiled at them. "Of course you didn't. You two may spend recess playing games on the computer."

"Fine with me," Cassidy said. "I don't have any friends I want to spend recess with anyway."

"I don't even want to be on the same playground as you," Jeff muttered.

Nina couldn't stand that her two best friends in the world were fighting. She didn't know what to do, but she did know that the tattletale was ruining a great friendship and was keeping her from playing soccer on the playground. That meant one thing: She had to find out who the tattler was and make them pay!

6
Cracking the Case

At the end of the day, Cassidy and Jeff stalked up the steps and out of the classroom. They hadn't said a single word to each other all day. They had been so mad, they hadn't even paid attention to the ghosts.

Nina caught up with them on the playground. "We have to talk," she told them.

"I'm not talking to her," Jeff said, pointing at Cassidy. "She told everybody I was scared of rabbits."

"And I'm not talking to him *ever again*," Cassidy said, nodding in Jeff's direction. "He told everyone I loved Mr. Morton."

"But you're blaming each other for something you know didn't happen," Nina told them.

"How can you be sure Cassidy didn't send that stuff to Justin Thyme?" Jeff asked.

"Because she wouldn't have included a secret about herself," Nina said logically. "And she didn't write that bunny thing on the flip chart because she was with us when that happened. Neither one of you is the classroom blabbermouth, so you might as well stop being mad at each other."

"Well, if Cassidy didn't do it and I didn't do it, then who did?" Jeff asked.

"I haven't figured that out yet," Nina said, "but one thing is for sure: Somebody is spying on us and it's getting us in trouble. All of us."

A spy was in their midst and Cassidy didn't like it one bit. After all, Cassidy planned on being a famous computer spy for the FBI when she grew up. It didn't look good that a tattletale was spilling secrets right under her nose. "What are we going to do about it?" she asked.

Nina pulled Cassidy and Jeff over to the monkey bars. Then Nina looked Cassidy right in the eyes. "You're the one that wants to be a computer spy. Now is your chance to crack your first case. What would a spy do?"

Cassidy nodded with new determination. Nina was right. Cassidy tossed her book bag on the ground and pulled out a plain blue notebook. "We need to think about what we already know," she said. "Sometimes when you write everything down, you see a pattern that leads to the bad guy."

Jeff and Nina looked over Cassidy's shoulder. "Your journal isn't nearly as sparkly as Carla's and Darla's," Jeff told her.

"It's not what's on the cover that counts," Cassidy said. "It's what's on the inside." She opened to a fresh page and made a list of suspects. She wrote Andrew at the top of the page.

"I bet it's Andrew," Nina said with a nod. "He's such a bully. This is definitely something he would do."

"But the tattler told a huge secret about him, too," Jeff said. "Besides, he isn't smart enough to do something like this."

Cassidy put a line through Andrew's name and listed Barbara's name. "Tattler told on her, too," Nina pointed out. "So it can't be her."

Cassidy crossed out her name and tried

another, but everybody she wrote down couldn't be the blabbermouth for one reason or another. Soon her page was filled with crossed-out names. "All we have is a page full of wrong answers," Cassidy groaned.

"There are two people that haven't gotten in trouble," Nina said slowly. "Carla and Darla."

"They never get in trouble," Jeff pointed out.

Cassidy nodded. "That's because they're too busy telling Mr. Morton what we're doing."

"Exactly," Nina said. "They're natural born tattletales and now they've taken it to a professional level."

Cassidy had watched lots of crime shows. She knew identifying suspects didn't solve the case. "We can't blame them without proof," Cassidy told Nina.

"Then we have to get proof," Nina said. "Let's figure out what we do know."

Cassidy started a new list.

1.) Someone is telling our secrets.
2.) They sent information to Justin Thyme.
3.) Justin announced it to the whole school in his article.
4.) Carla and Darla are the only two kids who haven't gotten in trouble.

"That doesn't look like very much to go on," Jeff said.

"But it's all we've got," Nina said. "It must contain the one clue we need."

"There are no clues there," Jeff said. He tapped his foot, eager to get moving.

"Yes, there is," Nina said suddenly, jumping up and down. "The clue is *The Legend*. All we have to do is track down evidence of Justin Thyme's mysterious source, and then we'll find the culprit."

"Maybe there isn't a source," Jeff suggested. "Justin Thyme could be making all this up just to get headlines."

"I know how we can find out," Nina said.

"How?" Cassidy and Jeff asked at the same time.

"By being what Cassidy has always wanted to be," Nina said. "Spies."

7
Spying Mission

The next morning the kids walked to school so early that the street lights hadn't shut off yet. The sun peeked out over the rooftops, but just barely. Their backpacks were full of things other than homework.

"Are we ready?" Nina asked softly. No one else was on the playground, but it was so quiet she felt like she needed to whisper.

Jeff and Cassidy nodded. Jeff took a black ski mask out of his backpack and put it on. Nina pulled out a kitty-cat flashlight. Cassidy slipped on the night vision goggles she had received for her birthday. "How do we get inside without getting caught?" Jeff asked.

"Simple," Cassidy said. "Follow me." She led Nina and Jeff through the school's unlocked back door to *The Legend*'s newspaper office—which just happened to be a small closet next to the principal's office. Thankfully, no lights were on yet in the office.

Nina switched on her flashlight and Cassidy clicked on the green glow of her night vision glasses. Nina thought they made Cassidy look a little bit like a

ghost. The kids slowly cracked open the door to the newspaper room.

"What exactly are we looking for?" Jeff asked.

"Notes that Justin got from Carla and Darla," Nina whispered. She opened a file drawer that was mostly filled with printed copies of the online newspaper.

"Look at this," Nina said when she looked in the bottom drawer.

"Is it from Carla and Darla?" Cassidy asked, leaning over Nina's shoulder and casting a green glow on the folder in Nina's hands.

"No," Nina said. "It's about local legends."

"We should've known better than to trust a newspaper named after tall tales," Cassidy said.

Jeff agreed. "Newspapers are only supposed to report the facts after checking to make sure their sources are telling the truth."

"If that was the case," Cassidy said, "movie magazines would go out of business."

"This is neat stuff, though," Nina said as she leafed through the papers in the folder. "Did you know that Sleepy Hollow had its very own bandit? Her name was Amy Lou Marple. She lived around the time the first Sleepy Hollow Elementary was still a one-room schoolhouse."

"We don't have time to read fairy tales," Cassidy told her. "We're looking for clues that could save us from a lifetime of detention."

"But these legends are about Sleepy Hollow," Nina said. "They're interesting."

Cassidy grabbed the paper out of Nina's hand and stuffed it into her backpack. "You can read it as a bedtime story tonight," Cassidy told her friend. "Now help look for clues to our blabber-mouth!"

The kids were so busy searching the room, they didn't notice a tall shadow darkening the doorway . . . until it was too late.

8
Busted

Ms. Finkle, their principal, tapped her long painted fingernails on the door frame. The kids turned and stared. Nina stuttered, "We . . . we . . ."

Cassidy stammered as she pulled off the night vision goggles. "We . . . um . . . we . . ."

Jeff, who was as quick with a fib as he was in a footrace, saved them all. "We were doing Justin Thyme a favor," Jeff told Ms. Finkle, "and dropping off a piece of paper."

Ms. Finkle glared over her half-glasses as if she didn't believe him.

Jeff jabbed Nina in the side. "Go ahead," Jeff said. "Put it where Justin told you."

Nina looked at Jeff as if he had just sprouted spinach for hair.

"Remember?" Cassidy prodded. "It's in your book bag."

Nina blinked. "Oh! Yeah!" She reached in her pack and pulled out the copy of the Sleepy Hollow bandit legend. Carefully, Nina put it back in the folder where she had found it.

Ms. Finkle frowned, but she finally nodded. "I'm heading down to your room," she said. "I understand there is an emergency. Walk with me."

The kids gulped. Did the ghosts do something terrible? Nina, Cassidy, and Jeff had no choice but to follow their principal into the hall. Nina saw by the wall clock that it was almost time for school to start. The minutes had flown by during their failed espionage mission.

They followed Ms. Finkle down the steps and into the dingy basement. The rest of their class was already there. Mr. Morton's face drained of color when he saw Ms. Finkle at the door. He was not the only one that looked nervous.

The classroom ghosts took one look at Ms. Finkle and scrambled. Becky and Sadie oozed into desks. Nate squeezed into Mr. Morton's coffee cup. Ozzy hid in the math box. Edgar had been perched on the computer. He slammed shut his journal and sat up straight. Cassidy noticed he had used chalk to draw a white star on the plain brown cover of his journal. Calliope grabbed her cat and they both disappeared into the tiny holes of her ghost fiddle. Huxley dashed around the room, looking for a place to go. Finally, he dove into the trash can until only his tail showed.

"Principals do that," Jeff whispered. "They make *everyone* nervous."

The worst sight of all was Carla and Darla. They sat at their desks with their heads down. It looked like they were crying. And then Nina saw why. There, in huge purple chalk letters written across the floor, was something so terrible that Nina shuddered.

CARLA AND DARLA SWIPED STARS

The corners of Cassidy's mouth twitched. She covered her mouth with her hands, pinching her lips so nobody could see her smile at the thought of the

CARLa and DaRLa SWIPed STARs

world's biggest goody two-shoes getting caught stealing stars from Mr. Morton's desk.

Ms. Finkle marched to the front of the room. She took her time examining each purple letter. Then, slowly, she turned and eyeballed every kid in the room until they squirmed.

"I understand this class needs a lesson in rules," Ms. Finkle finally said. "Perhaps this will help you remember them. The basement class of Sleepy Hollow Elementary *will* behave or there will be no recess for the entire month!"

9
Deep Doo-Doo

For the rest of the morning, the third graders didn't make a peep. Not even Carla and Darla. They were too afraid of Ms. Finkle's warning. Not the ghosts, though. They acted as if they were at a party. They danced and zoomed around the room. Even Edgar, who usually didn't mingle with the other ghosts, did a little jig above Mr. Morton's desk.

Finally, recess time came. Mr. Morton cleared his throat. "We will *try* having recess today," he said. "But don't think I've forgotten Ms. Finkle's warning. One *hint* of a problem and that's it for a month."

The kids quietly lined up and filed out the door that led straight to the playground. Nina pulled Jeff and Cassidy to the monkey bars. Not too many kids played on them, so it was the perfect place for the three friends to talk without being overheard.

"The tattler got Carla and Darla," Nina said at recess. "So the twins obviously aren't the culprits."

"They were really upset," Jeff agreed. "I felt kind of sorry for them."

"Whoever is doing this had better stop," Nina said, "or we'll never have recess again!"

"What I can't figure out," Cassidy said, "is the motive. Every spy knows criminals have to have a reason for doing their horrible deeds."

"Why would someone want to make everyone miserable?" Jeff asked.

Nina gasped. "Not *everyone* is miserable," she said slowly.

"Yes, they are," Cassidy said. "Just look at them."

The three friends glanced around the playground. Usually recess was noisy with kids kicking soccer balls, jumping ropes, and playing dodge ball. Not today. Instead, kids were clustered in small groups, heads down, talking in whispers.

"You're right. The *kids* of the basement room aren't happy," Nina said with a nod. "But the *ghosts* are just fine."

The bell rang ending recess. Cassidy, Jeff, and Nina jumped down from their perch on the monkey bars and slowly made their way toward Mr. Morton.

"That's for sure. The ghosts are having a great time," Jeff said. He was still mad at the way Ozzy had made fun of him that morning.

"Exactly," Nina said, as Mr. Morton led the class down to the shadows of the basement. "That's why I think the ghosts are the culprits behind this tattletale mess."

Cassidy slapped her forehead. Why hadn't she thought of that? "If what you say is true," Cassidy said, "then we're in for big trouble. There is no reason for the ghosts to stop!"

"I think we're too late," Nina said as they walked into the damp- ness of their class- room. "Look!"

There, flashing

Ms. Finkle Hates Kids.

on the computer screen, was a secret that made them all gasp.

Ms. Finkle hates kids.

"We are in deep doo-doo now," Jeff said.

10
Something Stinky

Mr. Morton wiped the chalk dust from his glasses. He peered at the computer. Then he turned and looked at his class. "This has gone too far," he said. "Recess has been canceled. Forever!"

Andrew groaned. Nina gasped. Even Carla and Darla looked like they might cry again.

But the ghosts didn't seem upset. Ozzy zoomed to the front of the room and stared at the stickers on Mr. Morton's desk. Nina knew ghosts had to think hard to touch things in the real world, so she knew Ozzy was concentrating harder than usual when he plucked a star from the sheet and flew across the room to stick it smack-dab on the middle of Edgar's journal. She was glad no one

noticed the single gold star flying through the air.

Edgar swelled at the sight of the shiny star on his journal. He puffed out his chest until it was three times bigger than usual.

"What are we going to do?" Nina asked in a shaky voice. "The ghosts are out of control!"

"There is nothing we can do," Cassidy said. "Nobody can stop them."

"Well, at least we know it can't get much worse," Jeff muttered.

But Jeff was wrong. Very wrong.

After lunch Mr. Morton wrote science questions on the board. He raised the old-timey map, and there, another secret was written in shaky green letters.

OZZY FLUNKED SPELLING

"Who is Ozzy?" Andrew wondered out loud.

The kids in the classroom whispered, "Is it someone's brother? Somebody's middle name?"

Only Cassidy, Jeff, and Nina knew — and, of course, the rest of the ghosts.

Ozzy took one look at the writing and roared. His green form turned gray and he zoomed around the room like an angry tornado. Jeff ducked. Cassidy slid down in her desk. Nina covered her head as papers flew from desks.

Mr. Morton looked up from his grade book. "Please close the doors and windows," he said to Carla and Darla. "The wind must really be blowing outside."

The next morning things were even worse.

BECKY FEARS THE DARK

was scrawled across Mr. Morton's grade book in thick red ink.

Carla and Darla stared at the grade book in shock. "Mr. Morton will . . ." Darla said.

". . . be so mad," Carla agreed.

"We have to fix it . . ." Darla started.

". . . before he gets here," Carla finished. The girls took their fat blue erasers and turned the red words into a pink smudge.

"Who's Becky anyway?" Andrew asked. "And why is she such a baby?"

"That's not true," Becky cried, but Andrew didn't hear her. She was so mad she hit Mr. Morton's desk. Only she forgot to concentrate and her ghostly fist sank into the wood all the way up to her elbow. She let loose with a blood-curdling scream that broke the ghost-sound barrier that usually only Cassidy, Jeff, and Nina could hear. The whole class froze.

Just then the kids heard a jingle. Or maybe it was a jangle. The classroom door crashed open. There stood Olivia.

Olivia had been Sleepy Hollow's janitor since before even their parents could remember. She had a soft spot for lost and homeless critters — and not just the cute furry kind. "Webster and I smell something a little stinky in here," Olivia said. "Thought we should check it out since Mr. Morton is still in an early morning meeting."

The rest of the class stared at the striped animal on Olivia's shoulder and carefully moved as far away as possible. When the skunk sniffed the air, his tail twitched twice. Then Webster scurried down the back of Olivia's red overalls, jumped to the floor, and disappeared back down the dark hallway.

"Yep. Something's stinky in this class-room," Olivia said. "Even Webster sensed it."

Darla cleared her throat and explained that they were having a problem with storytelling.

"Yeah," Andrew said, "some jerk is writing mean stuff everywhere."

Olivia nodded her head and her ear-rings clinked. Or maybe they clanked. "Some storytellers get confused between the stories they tell and the praise they get for the telling."

Olivia looked right at Carla and Darla when she said it. The twins looked down at their spelling worksheets.

"Maybe the one with all the stories to tell needs a better way of getting atten-tion!" Olivia looked around the room until her eyes found Jeff. "You know about storytelling," she said, "like those moving kind on film. You know that bad stories don't earn prizes."

Everyone, even Olivia, knew that Jeff

wanted to make movies when he grew up. "But I didn't do it," he sputtered. "I didn't tell on anyone."

Olivia didn't hear him. She had already turned and disappeared into the deep shadows of the hallway.

The class stared at Jeff. "I didn't do it," he said. "Really."

But nobody looked like they believed him.

11
Nightmare Ghost

All day long the rest of the class ignored Jeff. He was miserable. "Nobody believes me," Jeff said after school. He sat on the jungle gym with Cassidy and Nina.

"We know you didn't do it," Nina said.

Cassidy swung her legs back and forth. "It's the ghosts' fault."

"Wait a minute," Nina said slowly. "It can't be the ghosts. They're mad, too."

"Let's think about this," Nina continued. She clicked off the evidence on her fingers. "We know the culprit can't be Carla or Darla. It can't be Andrew. And it can't be Justin Thyme."

"How do you know?" Cassidy asked.

"Because, whoever the tattletale is knows about the ghosts," Nina said.

"That means it can be only one of three people. And we're all standing right here," Jeff said.

"We know we didn't do it," Cassidy said.

"Olivia said something that reminded me of one person we haven't thought of," Nina said, jumping off the jungle gym. "There is one *real* writer in the haunted basement of Ghostville Elementary. Edgar!"

"Edgar the ghost?" Cassidy asked. "But why would he do it?"

"I think I know," Jeff said. "He's doing all this to get story ideas, and then he's sending them to Justin Thyme so he can get them printed."

Nina nodded. "Haven't you noticed? Every time something happens, Edgar starts writing in his journal."

"That means that notebook is full of stuff about us," Jeff said, his face grim.

"What are we going to do about it?" Cassidy asked.

68

Nina didn't answer. She hurried across the playground and straight down the steps to the basement of Ghostville Elementary. Cassidy and Jeff followed her.

Nina stood in front of the picture hanging on the classroom wall. There sat Edgar, writing away in his journal. Nina knocked on the glass to get his  attention. Edgar oozed out of the picture.

When he did, Jeff grabbed for Edgar's journal. Jeff's hand passed right through it, but the book was knocked from Edgar's grasp. Edgar somersaulted after it. Cassidy was faster. She used a math book to fan it toward Nina. The journal rippled through the air. "Don't let him get it," Cassidy screamed.

Edgar bore down on Nina like a freight

train. Nina opened her mouth to scream. When she did, Edgar's journal flew right into her mouth.

Edgar turned into a worst-nightmare kind of ghost. "GIVE IT BACK," he roared. The wind from his words caused a thundercloud of black air to swirl around the room.

Nina closed her mouth, her cheeks puffed out to make room for the ghostly book.

"Swallow it, Nina," Jeff said. "That way Edgar will never be able to show our stories to anyone again."

"Don't! If you eat it, my words will be lost forever," Edgar shouted. "Why are you doing this to me?"

"Because you told on us," Jeff yelled back. His words sounded tiny compared to Edgar's.

"I don't know what you're talking about!" Edgar howled.

None of the kids noticed the green

sparkles twinkling behind them. The sparkles turned into five curious ghosts.

"What's going on here?" Ozzy asked.

"She stole my life's work," Edgar moaned.

Ozzy, Becky, Sadie, Nate, and even Calliope stared at Nina in disbelief. "How could you?" Sadie gasped. Sadie liked to think that she and Nina were best friends.

Nina couldn't talk. Her cheeks wiggled as Edgar's journal shifted in her mouth.

Cassidy answered for her. "He's the one who's been writing those horrible things about everyone. He's putting it all in his journal."

Edgar shook his head. "I am not the one."

"You're lying," Jeff snapped.

Ozzy shook his head. "Edgar never lied," he said simply. "He isn't the one."

"If Edgar didn't do it," Cassidy asked, "then who did?"

12
Ghost Puddle

"I didn't do it," Ozzy said.

"Don't look at me," Becky said. "I hate to write."

"I'm not very good at telling stories," Sadie admitted.

Calliope shrugged her thin ghost shoulders. "I'd rather play the violin than write silly notes."

Cassidy put her hands on her hips and frowned. "Well, someone has been writing not-so-nice things about all of us."

Nina noticed that Nate had his head down, looking at his bare feet. She tapped Jeff on the shoulder, then pointed at the quiet ghost.

"Nate," Jeff asked, "was it you? Did you write those things?"

Nate didn't say a word and Jeff asked again. "Nate, did you write those bad things?"

Nate nodded.

"You told on us!" Ozzy bellowed as he and the other ghosts slowly advanced toward Nate.

Nina's knees were shaking. She couldn't believe Nate would do something so mean. She knew the ghosts were mad. Everybody was mad. But she didn't want to see a ghost fight break out in the middle of her classroom.

The other ghosts got closer and closer to Nate. Nina worried that it would be the end of the quietest ghost in their school. She was so nervous she hiccupped. Cassidy slapped her hand over Nina's mouth, but Edgar's journal slipped through Cassidy's fingers. Edgar quickly grabbed his book.

"Don't hurt him," Nina blurted. "Telling isn't always bad." Everybody, ghosts and kids, glared at Nina.

Becky floated over to Nate and put her hand on his shoulder. "Why did you do it?" she asked.

Nate spoke for the first time the kids could remember. His voice was soft and shy. "I . . . I really like Edgar's stories. He's going to be famous someday for his writings." Nate kicked his bare toe onto the classroom floor.

Edgar's glasses sparkled. "You think I'm going to be famous?"

Nate shrugged again. "Words are powerful. People paid attention to what I wrote."

"Words *are* powerful," Nina admitted, feeling a bit sorry for Nate, "but some things are private."

"You told secrets!" Ozzy huffed. "Miss Hinkleberry would have taken you out to the woodshed for a spanking. That's exactly what you need now."

Ozzy's fist turned into a long wooden paddle. Nate pushed away the paddle and

a ghost battle began. The two ghosts rolled around the classroom, toppling desks and sending math papers flying.

Nina knew she had to talk fast. "Stop!" Nina screamed. "Nobody's perfect. Even I make mistakes."

"Nooooo," Sadie moaned. "What did you do?"

Nina thought earlier in the week and it suddenly struck her. "Carla and Darla wanted to play soccer, but I didn't want them on my team," Nina said. "I picked everybody else until Carla and Darla were the last ones left.

"Soooooo saaaaaad," Sadie said.

Nina gasped. She hadn't meant to be mean. Nina made a promise to herself to be nicer.

Ozzy and Nate stopped fighting when Becky stepped between them. "Nate wasn't perfect, either," Becky said.

"That's right," Ozzy said with a wicked smile. "Nate sucked his thumb!"

"Noooooooo!" Nate screeched. "Don't tell!"

Nate melted into a puddle on the floor. Nina nudged the puddle with her toe. "What if we all stop telling bad things about one another and just be nice?"

Nina looked at Jeff. "Say something good about Nate," she said.

Jeff shrugged. "You make a great blob on the floor."

Nina rolled her eyes and looked at Cassidy. "Say something else."

"You are the most peaceful ghost I know," Cassidy said slowly. "And I bet you can write other things and become famous."

The green puddle on the floor that was Nate bubbled.

Becky nodded. "As long as you write things that aren't mean."

Nate bubbled a little more.

Edgar bent over and dipped his pencil in Nate's puddle. "I'll help you. We can write stories together."

Nate bubbled and boiled until his head poked up from the puddle. "Really?" he asked.

Edgar nodded. "Really."

Nate started to spin until the puddle became solid and Nate was back to his

ghostly old self. "Just think of the stories we can write," Nate said.

"My favorite books are written by two ladies who write together," Nina added.

"Those are good. They should make movies about those books." Jeff smiled. "In this one movie I saw called *Ghost Writer*, everything the ghost wrote came true."

Nate's eyes sprung out of his head. "Ooooh, that sounds fun."

Nina got a sick feeling in her stomach. Stories that came true. That sounded dangerous. "Wait just a minute," she yelled at Nate and Edgar. But she was too late; they had already slipped themselves into Edgar's picture.

Cassidy gulped and stared at the two ghosts huddling over Edgar's journal. "Do you think their stories could really come to life?" she asked.

Nina shuddered. "Maybe not at an ordinary school. But at Ghostville Elementary, anything could happen!"

Ready for more spooky fun?
Then take a sneak peek at the next

Ghostville Elementary®

#10 Class Trip to the Haunted House

Andrew didn't bat an eye. "I'm not moving away," he said. "I'll still be living in Sleepy Hollow and going to school here."

"Rats," Jeff muttered and slid down in his seat until his chin rested on his old-fashioned desk. . . .

"In fact," and here, Andrew puffed out his chest and *really* started to brag, "my family is moving into the biggest house in town."

"That would be the Blackburn Estate," Nina gasped.

"Exactly," Andrew said. "My mother just inherited so much money I'm going to be the richest kid in town."

"The Blackburn Estate is falling down," Cassidy blurted out. "Why would you want to live there?"

"My dad plans on turning the Blackburn Estate into the biggest and bestest mansion this side of the Mississippi," Andrew said. "Dad's going to tear most of it down and rebuild it."

At his words, a scream ripped through the air and echoed down the halls, bringing the class to a dead stop. . . .

Usually Cassidy, Jeff, and Nina didn't see Calliope the ghost very much, except when she played her violin and sang songs with notes that didn't quite match. But when they heard the scream, they knew exactly which ghost it was coming from. Calliope's scream was as off-key as her singing. It ripped through the air and bounced off the walls. It rattled the windows and made Huxley, the ghost dog, jump so high his head went through Mr. Morton's desk.

Nina put her fingers in her ears. Cassidy yelped. Jeff fell out of his chair. Jeff knew it took tremendous ghost energy — and something very important — to break the ghost-sound barrier so that everyone could hear. Calliope's scream did just that.

The entire class erupted in shouts and squeals.

Carla jumped up from her seat in the front row. "Is somebody . . ."

". . . hurt?" her twin sister Darla finished.

Mr. Morton pushed back his chair so fast it toppled over. "Stay in your seats," Mr. Morton yelled over his shoulder as he rushed into the hallway to see if someone needed help.

Five kids hopped up from their seats

and followed Mr. Morton. Three more kids swung open the back door that led straight outside and to the playground.

"Hey!" Andrew blurted. "Where's everybody going? I was in the middle of my story. I haven't gotten to the part about how much this is going to cost. You'll never believe it. Come back here!"

"It looks like your story has come to a *screeching* halt," Jeff said with a satisfied grin. "As soon as Mr. Morton comes back, it'll be my turn."

Andrew curled his fingers into a fist. "This is your fault, isn't it?" he asked. "You used some special movie effect to interrupt me before I got to the best part."

No sooner were the words out of his mouth than the musical ghost named Calliope floated down the aisle between Nina and Cassidy. Calliope's long dark braid floated above her head. Her cat, Cocomo, reached up to swat at Calliope's dress, but the ghostly claws went right through the flowing fabric.

Calliope gazed straight ahead as if she didn't see anything else in the room. She looked different than usual. Her color had turned to a sickly shade of yellow and her eyes glowed green like mushy peas.

The rest of the ghosts noticed, too. They hurried out of Calliope's way, going straight through desks and chairs. Calliope stopped next to Andrew in the front of the room. Andrew didn't have a clue that a ghost had appeared next to him.

Calliope opened her mouth to speak, but nothing came out. Her eyes got big and the yellow of her skin deepened to the color of a rotten banana. Her green eyes watered like a swamp, but she didn't cry.

Again, she opened her mouth to speak. Not a single word came. It was as if somebody, or something, had silenced Calliope forever.

Creepy, weird, wacky, and
funny things
happen to the
Bailey School Kids!™
Collect and read them all!

The Adventures of THE BAILEY SCHOOL KIDS®

The Adventures of

THE BAILEY SCHOOL KIDS®

- ☐ 0-439-04397-2   **#37**   **Goblins Don't Play Video Games** ....$3.99 US
- ☐ 0-439-04398-0   **#38**   **Ninjas Don't Bake Pumpkin Pie** ....$3.99 US
- ☐ 0-439-04399-9   **#39**   **Dracula Doesn't Rock and Roll** ....$3.99 US
- ☐ 0-439-04401-4   **#40**   **Sea Monsters Don't Ride Motorcycles** ....$3.99 US
- ☐ 0-439-04400-6   **#41**   **The Bride of Frankenstein Doesn't Bake Cookies** ....$3.99 US
- ☐ 0-439-21582-X   **#42**   **Robots Don't Catch Chicken Pox** ....$3.99 US
- ☐ 0-439-21583-8   **#43**   **Vikings Don't Wear Wrestling Belts** ....$3.99 US
- ☐ 0-439-21584-6   **#44**   **Ghosts Don't Rope Wild Horses** ....$3.99 US
- ☐ 0-439-36803-0   **#45**   **Wizards Don't Wear Graduation Gowns** ....$3.99 US
- ☐ 0-439-36805-7   **#46**   **Sea Serpents Don't Juggle Water Balloons** ....$3.99 US
- ☐ 0-439-55999-5   **#47**   **Frankenstein Doesn't Start Food Fights** ....$3.99 US
- ☐ 0-439-56000-4   **#48**   **Dracula Doesn't Play Kickball** ....$3.99 US
- ☐ 0-439-65036-4   **#49**   **Werewolves Don't Run For President** ....$3.99 US
- ☐ 0-439-65037-2   **#50**   **The Abominable Snowman Doesn't Roast Marshmallows** .$3.99 US

- ☐ 0-439-40831-8   **Bailey School Kids Holiday Special:**
  Aliens Don't Carve Jack-o'-lanterns ....$3.99 US
- ☐ 0-439-40832-6   **Bailey School Kids Holiday Special:**
  Mrs. Claus Doesn't Climb Telephone Poles ....$3.99 US
- ☐ 0-439-33338-5   **Bailey School Kids Thanksgiving Special:**
  Swampmonsters Don't Chase Wild Turkeys ....$3.99 US
- ☐ 0-439-40834-2   **Bailey School Kids Holiday Special:**
  Ogres Don't Hunt Easter Eggs ....$3.99 US
- ☐ 0-439-40833-4   **Bailey School Kids Holiday Special:**
  Leprechauns Don't Play Fetch ....$3.99 US

Available wherever you buy books, or use this order form.

- -

Scholastic Inc., P.O. Box 7502, Jefferson City, MO 65102

Please send me the books I have checked above. I am enclosing $_____ (please add $2.00 to cover shipping and handling). Send check or money order — no cash or C.O.D.s please.

Name _____

Address _____

City _____ State/Zip _____

Please allow four to six weeks for delivery. Offer good in the U.S. only. Sorry, mail orders are not available to residents of Canada. Prices subject to change.